Hairy Monster

in

I Spy Scary Monsters

Scholastic Children's Books
Scholastic Publications Ltd
7-9 Pratt Street, London NW1 0AE, UK

Scholastic Inc
730 Broadway, New York, NY 10003, USA

Scholastic Canada Ltd
123 Newkirk Road, Richmond Hill
Ontario, Canada L4C 3G5

Ashton Scholastic Pty Ltd
PO Box 579, Gosford, New South Wales
Australia

Ashton Scholastic Ltd
Private Bag 1, Penrose, Auckland
New Zealand

First published by Scholastic Publications Ltd, 1993
Copyright © Frank Rodgers, 1993

ISBN: 0 590 55311 9

Typeset by Rapid Reprographics, London
Printed and bound in Belgium by Proost Book Production.

10 9 8 7 6 5 4 3 2 1

All rights reserved

The right of Frank Rodgers to be identified as the author of this work has been
asserted by him in accordance with the Copyright, Design and Patents Act, 1988.

This book is sold subject to the condition that it shall not, by way of trade or
otherwise be lent, resold, hired out, or otherwise circulated without the publisher's prior
consent in any form of binding or cover other than that in which it is published and
without a similar condition, including this condition, being imposed upon the
subsequent purchaser.

Hairy Monster

in
I Spy Scary Monsters

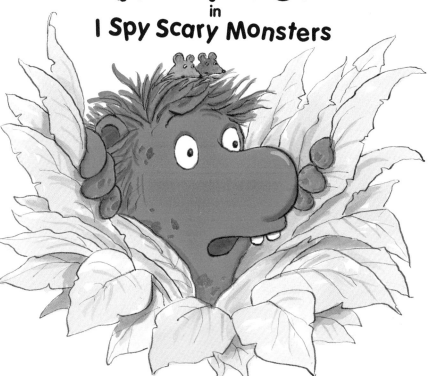

Frank Rodgers

Hairy Monster was always curious.
He loved to go rummaging in dark corners,
poking his nose into secret places just to
see what was going on.

He loved to wander through the swamp playing 'I spy'.

"I spy raspberries and blackcurrants," he cried and dived into an interesting bush. He came out an hour later licking his lips, and rubbing his tummy.

"I spy mud... delicious!" he exclaimed, and scrambled up a mossy bank to where there was a little pool of the special kind of mud that Monsters like to eat.

When he got back to the mud-mounds where
the Monsters lived he was covered in juice, mud,
leaves and moss.

Not only that, but in his long tangled hair he
had collected two field mice, a sparrow and
a hedgehog. They were enjoying the ride.

He was still playing 'I spy'.

As he passed Short-horned Monster's mud-
mound he popped his head in at the window.
"I spy stone and weed soup," he said, grinning
and licking his lips.

All Monsters love to share so Short-horned
Monster gave Hairy Monster a big bowl of stone
and weed soup with extra weeds.

At the next mud-mound Hairy Monster said,
"I spy smelly cheese!"

Furry Monster was delighted to share and gave
Hairy Monster a big, smelly slice.
"Yum," munched Hairy Monster.

Then he went to
the next mud-
mound where he got
delicious lumpy
custard balls...

then to the next
where he got
scrumptious
mud-loaf...

then to the next...and the next...
and the next...

"I spy stone and weed soup," said Hairy Monster.

Short-horned Monster blinked. "Again?"
he said. "You've been here before. Twice."
"I have?" asked Hairy Monster.

"Yes, you have," replied all the Monsters.
"You've been to all of us twice. If you 'I spy'
any more you'll burst!"

"In fact," they said, "don't play 'I spy' again
today in case you do!"

"But it's good fun...very!" protested Hairy
Monster.
"Good fun for you but a bit annoying for us,"
said the Monsters.

16

"Hm!" muttered Hairy Monster. "What a grumpy lot!" and stalked off into the swamp in a huff.

As he sat on a log wondering what to do next he heard a strange noise.

A snuffling, slithering, secret kind of noise. Hairy Monster was curious but remembered he wasn't supposed to play 'I spy' again.

His curiosity got the better of him however, and he parted the leaves to see what was going on.

"Oh!" he gasped in surprise. "I spy...

SCARY MONSTERS!"

Creeping sneakily through the swamp were
three fearsome-looking Wild Monsters. They
were heading for the mud-mounds.

"Oh no!" thought Hairy Monster. "They're planning to surprise the Monsters and steal our food! But what can I do? If I yell they'll grab me!"

Hairy Monster had an idea. He lifted the sparrow from his fur and whispered to it.

The sparrow whistled and flew into the air, making the Wild Monsters stop and look up.

While they were distracted, Hairy Monster
picked up the hedgehog and whispered to it too.

The hedgehog curled itself into a ball and
rolled...

right under the hand of the nearest Wild
Monster. "Yaaaoow!" yelled the Wild Monster as
he leant on the hedgehog.

"Shh!" hissed the other two. "Don't make so
much noise. They'll hear us!"

But Hairy Monster had whispered to the two field mice and now they ran up to the Wild Monsters.

"Boo!" they shrieked.

"Yaaa!" yelled the Wild Monsters in fright.
(Wild Monsters are scared of mice and spiders.)

"Yaahaa!" they shouted. "Mice! Horrible,
creepy, scary, tiny mice!"

The other Monsters heard the commotion and saw the Wild Monsters leaping about in the swamp.

"They're after our food again!" cried Long-horned Monster. "Let's give them some!"

Lumpy custard balls, slices of mud-loaf and bits of smelly cheese came whizzing through the air. SPLODGE! SPLOINK! SPLATTER!

"Yaaa!" yelled the Wild Monsters again. "Let's get out of here! Run for your lives!"

And they did.

When the Monsters found out that Hairy Monster's curiosity had saved them they were delighted.
"Play 'I spy' anytime!" they said.

That night they had a big party in honour of
Hairy Monster.

There was stone and weed soup, lumpy custard
balls, smelly cheese, mud-covered doughnuts and
mud-shakes.

Hairy Monster was still full after eating all afternoon so he only managed to eat...

three platefuls of soup, eight custard balls and thirteen mud-covered doughnuts before he fell asleep.

"Ah," laughed his friends, "We spy a sleeping Monster!"

So they gently lifted up Hairy Monster and carried him home to bed.